For Emma Layfield
with love and thanks, E.T.

Isabella's Toybox
by Emma Thomson

British Library Cataloguing in Publication Data
A catalogue record of this book is available from the British Library.

ISBN 97803 40893371

Isabella's Toybox © 2007 Emma Thomson.

First HB edition published 2007
2 4 6 8 10 9 7 5 3 1

Published by Hodder Children's Books,
a division of Hachette Children's Books,
338 Euston Road,
London,
NW1 3BH

Printed in China

Isabella's

Isabella's Toybox

Hee   haa

Tee-hee

Tee-hee

hee

h
Hodder
Children's
Books

A division of Hachette Children's Books

I knew a little girl called Isabella who had
a room full of toys but still wanted more!
She had new toys, old toys, fast toys,
pretty toys and spotty toys.

Isabella even had toys that
she'd forgotten all about...

Wish List
Jumping beans
Flip-flops
Bobble hat
Walkie-talkies
Lollipops
Dolly

Isabella's toybox sat snugly in the corner of her bedroom.
The key to the box had been lost many years ago.

Isabella's
Toybox

It was such a long time since the toybox
had been opened that the toys inside had forgotten
all about the outside.

Instead they made their own wonderful world inside,
full of special secrets.

It was the beginning of a new day and Rufus the cockerel woke the other toys up with a loud

cock-a-doodle-doo!

Notty the elephant woke up with a start.
"I wonder what today will bring?" she mumbled to the others.

"I hope today is like every other day!"
said Scribble the tortoise as he rolled onto his feet.

When Scribble wasn't sleeping, he loved to
fill his days drawing absolutely everywhere!
He was planning to cover the entire box with
magnificent, colourful doodles.

Oscar →

Henry

Notty

Rufus

Penny

Me

While Scribble was busy doodling, Oscar the giraffe made the other toys laugh with dizzy stories and silly jokes.

"When do giraffes have eight legs?"
chuckled Oscar.
"When there are two of them!"

Suddenly the toys heard Isabella
thundering up the stairs, two at
a time. They froze on the spot.

"What's happening?" squeaked Fidgit whose
little mouse ears hadn't heard a thing.

"Shhh! It's Isabella," whispered Blue the bear.
"She mustn't find out our secret. Keep still."

lollipops

"I've found it!" Isabella cried, running into
the room with the long lost key.

In the next moment, there was a loud clattering
noise and a stream of light flooded into the toybox.
The toys were bursting with excitement.

"Isabella!" they heard a voice call out.
"Come downstairs for tea."
And with a

thump,
thump,
thump,

she was gone.

Henry and Blue quickly jumped out of the box, followed by Fidgit, Scribble and Penny.

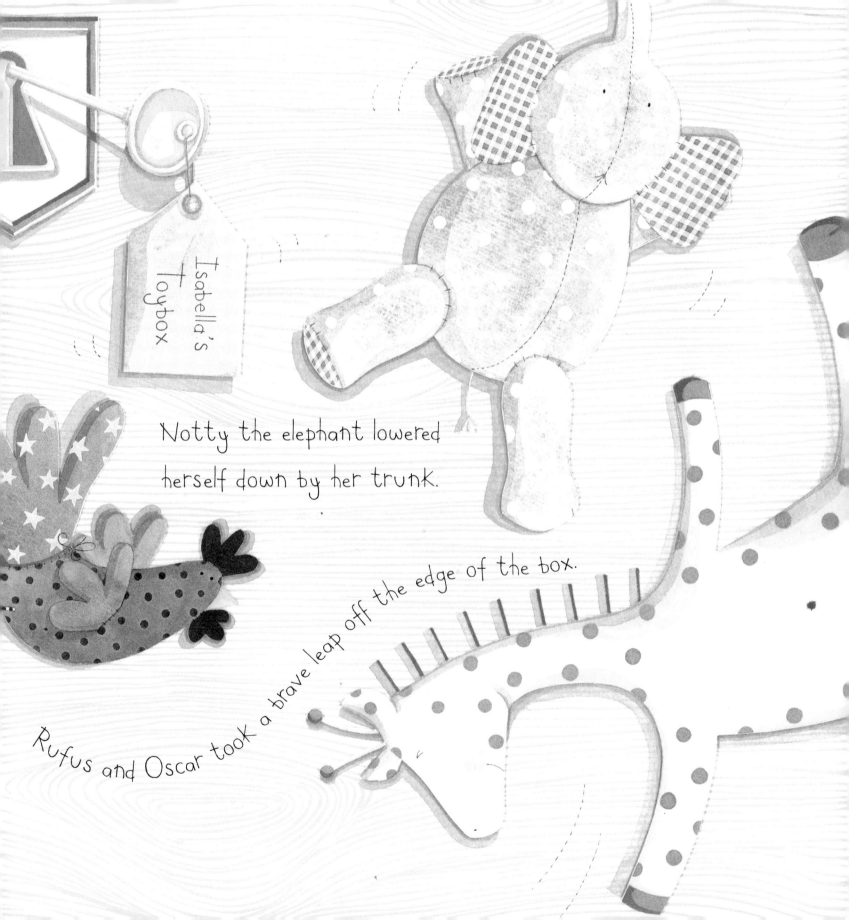

Isabella's Toybox

Notty the elephant lowered
herself down by her trunk.

Rufus and Oscar took a brave leap off the edge of the box.

The toys picked themselves
up and looked around.
They couldn't believe their eyes –
Isabella's bedroom was full of
amazing and exciting things!

"This is going to be so much fun!"
called out Notty as she jumped
onto the boat.

In fact, the toys were having so much fun
that they hadn't noticed the time flying by.
And none of them had seen Isabella who was
secretly watching them.

"My toys are real!" she gasped.

The toys heard the whisper and the slow creak of the door.
As quick as a flash, they jumped back into the box.

Wish List
Jumping beans
Flip-flops
Bobble hat
Walkie-talkies
Lollipops
Dolly

Ever so slowly, Isabella opened her bedroom door and walked over to the toybox. Carefully she took out the key and put it safely in her pocket with a soft pat.

Then she gently lifted out the toys. It was lovely to see her old friends again. How could she have forgotten them?

Now Isabella had new toys,

old toys,

fast toys,

pretty toys,

round toys,

spotty toys,

and best
of all...

real toys!